STANLEY & RHODA

by Rosemary Wells

DIAL BOOKS FOR YOUNG READERS
NEW YORK

For Jamie and Lottie

Published by
Dial Books for Young Readers
2 Park Avenue
New York, New York 10016

Copyright © 1978 by Rosemary Wells
All rights reserved. Design by Atha Tehon
Printed in Hong Kong by South China Printing Co.
C O B E
6 8 10 9 7 5

Library of Congress Cataloging in Publication Data
Wells, Rosemary.
Stanley and Rhoda.
Summary: In three episodes a brother and sister deal
with Rhoda's untidy room, a bee-sting, and a babysitter.
[1. Brothers and sisters—Fiction] I. Title.
PZ7.W46843St [E] 78-51874
ISBN 0-8037-8248-9
ISBN 0-8037-8249-7 (lib. bdg.)

CONTENTS

BUNNY BERRIES

"Rhoda, please clean up your room
now," said Rhoda's mother.

"Too tired," Rhoda answered.

"Stanley!" said their mother. "See that
Rhoda cleans up her room."

"Shake a leg, Rhoda," said Stanley.

"But, Stanley," said Rhoda, "where shall I begin?"

"Why don't you start by taking the beads out of your clay?" suggested Stanley.

"They're berries, not beads," said Rhoda.

"Whatever they are," said Stanley. "Rhoda, all your clothes are on the bed again."

"I'll put my berries in my berry bottle," said Rhoda.

"Help me make the bed, Rhoda," said Stanley.

"I call them bunny berries," said Rhoda, "because I feed them to my bunny."

"Well, there they go," said Stanley.
"Hand me that pillow please, Rhoda."
"I'll pick up the berries first," said
Rhoda.

"Your clay is stacked," said Stanley.
"Your bed is made, your clothes are
folded."
"And my berries are back in the jar,"
said Rhoda.

"Open the drawer for me please,
Rhoda," said Stanley.

"Are you ready, Rhoda?" called their
mother.

"Yes," answered Rhoda, "Stanley
helped."
"It was nothing," said Stanley.
"It's beautiful!" cried their mother.
"Hug and kiss please," said Rhoda.

"Hug and kiss and a cookie for both of you," said their mother.

"Come have your cookie, Stanley,"
called Rhoda.

"Okay," said Stanley.

DON'T TOUCH IT, DON'T LOOK AT IT

"Watch that bee!" Stanley advised.
"What bee?" asked Rhoda.
"Near your right foot," said Stanley.
"Which is my right?" asked Rhoda.

"The one with the freckle," said
Stanley.

"He got me!" Rhoda screamed.
"Wait a minute," said Stanley.
"It hurts!" Rhoda screamed.

"It's just a bee bite," said Stanley.
"It hurts!" Rhoda cried.
"Let me see it," asked Stanley.
"No!" said Rhoda.
"I just want to look," said Stanley.
"Don't touch it! Don't look at it!"
said Rhoda.

"Let's go home then," Stanley
suggested.

"I can't walk," said Rhoda.

Stanley took the rest of the rocks out
of the wagon and put Rhoda in.

"It hurts! It hurts!" Rhoda yelled.

"I know what," said Stanley.

"I'll put some nice cool mud on it."

Stanley fetched some mud.

"Dirty!" said Rhoda.
"Just try it," said Stanley.
"Don't touch it, don't look at it!"
said Rhoda.

"When we get home," said Stanley, "Daddy will fix it."

"What will Daddy do?" asked Rhoda.

"Take the bee sting out of your foot," Stanley answered.

"How?" Rhoda asked.

"Probably he'll use a needle," said Stanley.

"Or maybe tweezers," Stanley went
on. "Then again he might soak your
foot in boiling butter."

"On the other hand, he may just
decide to take you up to Doctor
Zuckerman and let him work on it
with his new splinter drill."

"It's better now, Stanley," said Rhoda.

"I'm glad," said Stanley.

"It will be perfect if you kiss it,"
said Rhoda.

"Nothing easier," said Stanley.

HENRY

"Stanley," said Stanley's mother, "this is Henry. He'll stay with you until I get back from the store."

"No!" said Rhoda.

"That's a little girl, isn't it?" asked Henry.

"No!" shouted Rhoda.

"Let's play ball," said Henry.
"I don't like you, Henry," said Rhoda.
"Give her a muffin, Henry,"
suggested Stanley. "It will cheer her up."
"Okay," said Henry.

"With jam or she won't eat it," said Stanley.

"Oh, yes," said Henry.

"More," said Rhoda.

"Say please, Rhoda," said Stanley. "Try ice cream, Henry."

"Oh, yes," said Henry.

"More," said Rhoda.

"Cake," Stanley suggested.
"Of course," said Henry.

"She needs a bath now, Henry,"
Stanley said.

"Oh, yes," said Henry.

"No bath!" shouted Rhoda.

"Yes," said Stanley.

"Here we go!" said Henry.
"Not that way, Henry," said Stanley.
"What way?" asked Henry.

"Don't you take your clothes off
when you get into a tub?" asked
Stanley.

"No!" Henry shouted.

"Never! I always take baths in my
clothes, even my football uniform!
Always!"

"Henry, I love you so much!" said
Rhoda.

"Don't cry, Henry," said Stanley.

"I'm home!" called their mother.

"Don't look!" said Henry.

"Don't be home yet!" said Rhoda.

"Is everybody all right?" asked their mother.

"Couldn't be better," said Stanley.